I0614753

Eleanor Donnelley

Little compliments of the season and other tiny rhymes for tiny readers

Eleanor Donnelley

Little compliments of the season and other tiny rhymes for tiny readers

ISBN/EAN: 9783337273118

Printed in Europe, USA, Canada, Australia, Japan

Cover: Foto ©Andreas Hilbeck / pixelio.de

More available books at **www.hansebooks.com**

Little Compliments of the Season,

AND OTHER

Tiny Rhymes for Tiny Readers.

SIMPLE VERSES, ORIGINAL, SELECTED, OR TRANSLATED,
FOR NAMEDAYS, BIRTHDAYS, CHRISTMAS, NEW-
YEAR, AND OTHER FESTIVE AND
SOCIAL OCCASIONS.

BY

ELEANOR C. DONNELLY.

NEW YORK, CINCINNATI, AND ST. LOUIS:

BENZIGER BROTHERS,

PRINTERS TO THE HOLY APOSTOLIC SEE.

1887.

DEDICATION.

To the Holy Innocents.

These little gems of Compliments,
    Of tiny Rhymes and true,
With love intense, sweet Innocents,
    We offer unto you.

In purer climes, these festal times,
    Be Childhood's gentle pleaders;
And while ye bless these tiny Rhymes,
    Bless, too, their tiny readers.

E. C. D

PHILADELPHIA :
    Feast of the Holy Innocents, 1885.

CONTENTS.

OTHER TINY RHYMES FOR TINY READERS.

I. *With the Babies.*

II. *At Play.*

Publishers' Preface.

THERE is probably no family or school that has not at some time felt the need of just such verses as are here offered.

On birthdays, Namedays (the feast of one's Patron Saint), Christmas, New-Year's, and other religious or domestic festivals the joyfulness of the occasion or the value of some trifling gift would be greatly enhanced if accompanied by a few well-chosen words suited to the capacity of a little child. But it is in vain we search for such; for though many are to be found in French and German, there is, as far as we know, nothing of the kind in English.

We feel, then, that we and the Catholic public are under no small obligation to the gifted lady who has consented to write or select these " Little Compliments of the Season." Almost every festival is here provided for; and by a simple change of a word or two the verses may be made to suit other occasions than those for which they were written.

In addition to the " Compliments," the author has, under the several titles of "With the Babies," "At Play," "At Work," and " At Prayer," given other pleasant rhymes, original or selected, which, we are satisfied, will be appreciated by the little ones for whom they are written. That all may prove useful and acceptable is the belief and hope of

THE PUBLISHERS.

Little Compliments of the Season.

The Youngest Child to the Family on Christmas Eve.

I'm very small,
Yet I wish to all,
On this sweet Christmas night,
Much happiness,
Much joy and bliss,
And a New Year merry and bright !

—From the German.

TO ONE'S PARENTS.

COME to the Crib, dear parents,
    As shepherds came of old,
To offer to the Holy Child
    The lambkins of your fold;

And our good Lord will bless them,
    And lead them in His way;
And from His shrine, the Babe Divine
    Will crown our Christmas Day!

ON CHRISTMAS MORNING.

Welcome, welcome, best of days !
    Holy feast and bright!
Shining through the cloudy year,
    Like a pleasant light.

CHRISTMAS! in thy very name
    Jesus seems to say:
" Little children, come and hear
    Mass on CHRISTMAS* Day!"

      * Christmas means Christ's mass.

CHILDREN TO THEIR PARENTS ON CHRISTMAS MORN- ING, WITH A GIFT OF FRUIT AND FLOWERS.

DEAR father, dear mother, pray tell us the cause
　Of that racket last night, and that knocking,
When, down the old chimney, the dear Santa Claus
　Came creeping to fill up each stocking.

You don't know the reason ? Then, while you stand
　　mute,
　We'll tell you this secret of ours :
Old Santa brought mother this basket of fruit,
　And you, dearest father, these flowers !

A Little Child to its Teacher on Christmas Eve.

To-DAY we close our happy school;
To-day we miss thy loving rule.

We part, but when vacation's o'er
We'll meet again, I hope, once more.

And ere we go, both girls and boys
Must wish thee all the season's joys.

A Christmas fair, a year of glee,
O teacher dear, we ask for thee !

To Grandmamma, with a Christmas Cake.

Dear grandma, while I make my bow
   Before thy easy-chair;
This Christmas Day to God we pray,
   To keep thee from all care.

I beg thee take this pretty cake,
   With all its ribbons gay,
And may this be, indeed, for thee,
   A merry Christmas Day !

To an Aunt.

Upon our charming Christmas tree
The blessed Christ-Child stands,
And gifts for thee, and gifts for me,
Are in His shining hands.

But oh ! the sweetest gift He brings,
Dear aunt, to thee and thine,
Was born with Him (the King of kings),—
A peace and love divine.

To a Brother, with a Christmas Box of Writing-Paper.

Here, dear brother, is a very
Useful gift of stationery.
On this paper, pure and white,
Purest thoughts your pen must write.

To a Sister, with a Vase.

If you have no flowers to place
In this pretty china vase,
Let, at least, your heart-vase be
Filled with flowers of piety.

To Grandpapa, with a Little Lamp.

This lovely little lamp be thine
To burn before our Lady's shrine.

To a Little Sister.

Let me wish thee, little love,
Every blessing from above.
This a happy Christmas be,
This a New Year bright for thee;
In the Christ-Child's peace divine,
Every joy and grace be thine!

With a Statue of St. Joseph.

The Foster-father of our Lord,
Our Blessed Lady's guide,—
Whatever grace you ask through *him*
Will never be denied.

To an Aunt, with the Gift of a Needle-case.

May this little useful gift
Your work-box, aunt, enrich,
And a wish of childish love
Go with every stitch.

To a Priest, from his Sunday-school Children, with a Gift of a Pyx-case.

A CASE for the holy Pyx,
  Wherein our Lord shall rest,
When borne to the suff'ring and the sick,
  Upon your priestly breast.

To-day, dear Reverend Father,
  Our Christmas off'ring take;
Our Lord will bless this sacred gift,
  Then wear it for His sake!

To an Orphan Cousin.

NOT "Merry Christmas!" will I say
To thee on this first Christmas Day
  Since thy dear parent's death;
But I will say, instead, to thee,
May Christmas Day most blessed be,
And all its hours (as fast they flee),
  Be full of peace and faith!

To One who has had Great Troubles.

THOUGH clouds across thy Christmas skies
  Have cast their shadows dark and drear,
May God's fair sunshine soon arise,
And light and peace from Paradise
  Make glad thy fresh New-Year!

A Little Child to his Grandfather or Grandmother.

Happy New-Year, grandpapa!
  Hear the sweet bells ringing;
Little angels, grandpapa,
  In the skies are singing.

Bells and angels, grandpapa,
  With your grandchild's greeting,
Happy New-Year, grandpapa!
  Are to-day repeating.

A Little Child's New-Year Wish to an Aunt.

This very little wish
With gladness I bring here:
  "Oh! may this be,
  Dear aunt, to thee,
A good and bright New-Year!"

—From the German.

To the Family.

Another spotless page is turned
  In the dusty book of Time;
And softly on the frosty air
  Rings out the New-Year's chime.

Let hearts grow glad, and eyes grow bright,
This merry winter morn;
Cast care away, and in the soul
Let peace and joy be born.

A LITTLE BOY TO HIS PARENTS.

BEHOLD a very little boy
Who wishes to you
here,
In simple words of heart-
felt joy,
A happy, bright New-
Year.

I know you will be very
glad
If now you find in me
A better and a wiser
lad
Than once I used to
be.

May Heaven grant you blest increase
Of joys ne'er known before;
And may God give you health and peace,
To-day, and evermore!

—*From the German.*

To Grandmamma on New-Year's Day.

On all thy ways God's blessing shine,
And quiet days be ever thine.

—From the German.

New-Year's Greeting to Parents who have Lost and Suffered Much.

That the New Year just beginning
  Shed upon you purest bliss ;
That it give you back the fulness
  Of your heart's lost happiness ;
And that Heaven, your life defending,
  Keep you from all grief and care,—
This, dear parents, is our greeting ;
  This, your little children's prayer.

—From the French.

A New-Year Wish.

Year after year,
  May God grant to you
Blessings most dear,
  And joys ever new !

—From the German

A LITTLE BOY'S NEW-YEAR WISH.

My dear little wish is as tiny as I,
  Two lines will express it to thee :
May kind Heaven bless thee! May kind
    Heaven keep thee,
  All healthy and merry for me !

—From the German.

Little Children to their Parents.

New-Year's Day has come at last,
And the Old Year safely passed ;
Dearest papa, mamma sweet,
Bless your children at your feet.
As a proof of tenderness,
And of simple happiness,
From these hearts obedient,
Take this humble compliment.

—From the French.

To Grandfather.

Dear grandpapa, the best of boys,
I come to wish you here
A Christmas full of sweetest joys,
A bright and glad New-Year.

With the Gift of a Cup

When you put this to your lips
And a draught of water drink,
While you bless your New-Year's gift,
Of its giver fondly think.

A Child to its Widowed Mother, the First New-Year's Day after its Father's Death.

Although in sorrow and distress
    We mourn with thee a father's loss,
A Heav'nly Father we possess,
    Who lightens every cross.

'Twas He who took our papa hence,
    But left us still a mother dear ;
And He will be the best of friends
    To bless our bright New-Year.

Then, dearest Mamma, let us lean
    In faith upon His loving arm ;
Our Father and our Friend unseen
    Will keep us from all harm.
                   —From the French.

Children to their Mother, with Birthday Flowers.

Before your birthday closes,
    Dear mother, here we bring
This basket of fresh roses,
    Affection's offering.

Accept this gift of ours,
    And may this morn of morns
Be like our lovely flowers
    In all things but the thorns !

𝕸𝖆𝖒𝖒𝖆'𝖘 𝕭𝖎𝖗𝖙𝖍𝖉𝖆𝖞 𝕭𝖔𝖚𝖖𝖚𝖊𝖙;

MADE UP BY PAPA FROM THE FAMILY FLOWERS.

PAPA SPEAKS: As this is Mamma's birthday,
　　　And *such* a charming day,
　At early dawn, upon the lawn,
　　　I plucked this large bouquet.
　They are the queerest flowers
　　　That e'er from garden came ;
　They run and walk, they laugh and talk,
　　　And each can tell its name.

FIRST CHILD : I am my Mamma's LILY,
  Her very heart's delight ;
  You need not think me silly
  Because I'm dressed in white.
  For this is Mamma's feast-day,
  And so her LILY tall
  Cries, "Happy, happy birthday !
  And Heaven bless us all !"

SECOND CHILD : I am my Mamma's PANSY,
  I'm nearly ten years old,
  And just to please her fancy,
  I dress in blue and gold.
  And on my mother's feast-day,
  Her PANSY loves to call,
  "Dear Mamma, happy birthday !
  And Heaven bless us all !"

THIRD CHILD : I am my Mamma's VIOLET,
  My purple hood hangs down ;
  And just like ev'ry violet,
  I wear a purple gown.
  To keep our pretty feast-day,
  I left the garden-wall,—
  Dear Mamma, happy birthday !
  And Heaven bless us all !

FOURTH CHILD : I am my Mamma's ROSEBUD,
  My scarlet dress is gay ;
  I'm such a little close bud,
  I haven't much to say.

But this is Mamma's feast-day,
And so her ROSEBUD small
Says, " Happy, happy birthday !
And Heaven bless us all !"

FIFTH CHILD : *I* am a LADY'S SLIPPER
    For darling Mamma's foot ;
I look so very *chipper*,
    I'm like a fairy's boot.
Who dances on our feast-day
    Will need *me* at the ball ;
Dear Mamma, happy birthday !
    And Heaven bless us all !

SIXTH CHILD : I am my Mamma's DAISY,
    Her darling little son ;
    You needn't think me crazy
    Because I'm full of fun.
    'Twould spoil my Mamma's feast-day
    If I should cry or squall,
    So, here's a happy birthday,
    And Heaven bless us all !

SEVENTH CHILD : My name is little BUTTERCUP,
    I wear a yellow suit ;
    I'm just an *awful* "cutter-up,"
    But still I'm rather cute.
    For fear I'd spoil the feast-day,
    They've kept me in the hall ;
    Dear Mamma, happy birthday !
    And Heaven bless us all !

EIGHTH CHILD : I am a blue FORGET-ME-NOT,
    My Papa loves me best ;
    I'm very small ; oh ! let me not
    Be lost among the rest.
    I bloom for ev'ry feast-day,
    In summer, spring, or fall,—
    Dear Mamma, happy birthday
    And Heaven bless us all !

NINTH CHILD : I am my Mamma's MIGNONETTE,
    Her little baby-boy.
    Because I'm such a little pet
    I fill the house with joy.

Dear Mamma, on your feast-day
    (Wrapped up in Nurse's shawl)
I wish you happy birthday,
    And Heaven bless us all !

PAPA CONCLUDES (*standing in the midst of the children*):

What *do* you think, dear Mamma,
    Of these bright buds of ours ?
        They run and walk,
        They laugh and talk,
    Like very funny flowers.

They've come to keep your birthday
From garden, wood, and water;
Then take to-day
Our sweet bouquet,
And bless each son and daughter !

To an Elder Brother, with a Birthday Gift.

HAPPY birthday, brother !
All the household here,
Father, too, and mother,
Wish you merry cheer.

Hold this box a minute ;
When its lid you lift,
You will find within it
Some one's birthday gift

Ha ! you like your present !
Now a smile—a kiss.
May each birthday pleasant
Be as glad as this !

WITH A BOUQUET.

'Tis true I'm very little,
　　But my love is very great :
I've gathered you these lilies
　　Beside the garden-gate.

With joy my face is glowing,
  My heart with pleasure burns.
A happy birthday, uncle,
  And many sweet returns!

A Child's Birthday Greeting to a Mother who has had Great Sorrows.

To-day, my darling Mamma,
  I venture to repeat
The tender prayers oft breathed for thee
  At Mary's holy feet.

Then drive away all sorrow,
  All care and sad distress,
And in my faithful love regain
  Your long-lost happiness.

—From the French.

A Very Little Boy to Papa on his Name-day.

Just see my little basket:
  Now don't you think it's cute?
'Tis dearest papa's name-day,
  And here's his fav'rite fruit.

O sweet St. N——— in heaven!
    I love your holy name,
I love your holy feast-day,
    'Cause papa's is the same.

Smile down, dear Saint, upon him,
    And bless his little boy;
And sweeter than this fruit shall be
    Each name-day full of joy !

A NAME-DAY GREETING TO AN AUNT.

My childish joys your love increased
    By ev'ry tender art.
Then, dearest aunt, upon your feast,
    Accept my grateful heart.
Oh ! more than words can ever tell,
    To give you joy I yearn;
I love you, aunt, I love you well,—
    Pray, love me in return !

                              —*From the French.*

AN EASTER WISH.

WHEN this Easter gift's untied
You will find a bird inside.

ANOTHER EASTER WISH.

THIS little Easter egg
With its tiny Rosary,
Is all the Easter gift
That I can give to thee.

WITH AN EASTER RABBIT.

THE little hare in this basket
Your kind indulgence begs.
He brings you these Easter wishes,
And plenty of Easter eggs.

A CHILD TO ITS FATHER AND MOTHER ON THEIR WEDDING ANNIVERSARY.

DEAREST parents, best of friends,
Ev'ry day I fondly pray
That your long and peaceful life
Free from care may pass away.

Little children's prayers, 'tis said,
Are most pleasing to the Lord.
May He, then, from heaven shed
On your hearts His best reward.

—From the French.

To Mamma on her Feast-Day.

Although a little child am I,
   It has occurred to me
To offer you this wish of mine—
   "Oh! may you happy be!"

             —From the German.

CHILDREN TO THEIR MOTHER ON HER RECOVERY FROM SICKNESS.

WHEN you were ill, dear mother,
Our hearts were very sad ;
Now you are well, dear mother,
Behold us gay and glad!

The days were dark and dreary
While vacant stood your chair;
Now everything looks cheery,
Because you're seated there.

This sweet bouquet, then, mother,
We offer with our song.
Oh! Heaven bless you, mother,
And keep you well and strong!

THE SAME TO A FATHER ON HIS RETURN FROM A JOURNEY.

WELCOME, welcome home once more!
Dearest father, here we stand,
Such a merry, happy band,
Waiting at the parlor-door.

All was sad before you came;
　Now our hearts with gladness leap,
　Now dear mamma will not weep
When the baby calls your name.

Draw the curtains, close the door,—
　Good old grandma's making tea;
　Every breast is full of glee,—
Dearest father's home once more!

SCHOOL-CHILDREN TO THEIR PASTOR ON HIS SILVER JUBILEE, PRESENTING A SILVER ALTAR-LAMP.

'Tis here, within this holy spot
　So full of peace and prayer,
The little children of the flock
　Have brought their off'ring rare.

A silver lamp whose gentle light
　And never-failing ray
Shall be a star-beam for the night,
　A sunbeam for the day.

O'er aisle and altar it will shed
　Its lustre soft and warm;
'Twill shine upon each bended head,
　And on each kneeling form.

And as that bright and beaming Star,
 In ages passed away,
Led Eastern Magi from afar
 To where the Saviour lay,

So may our lamp, a star in air,
 Both saints and sinners greet,
And lead them on, in faith and prayer,
 To kiss their Saviour's feet!

SUNDAY-SCHOOL CHILDREN TO A PRIEST (RELIGIOUS SISTER OR BROTHER), ON THE OCCASION OF A GOLDEN JUBILEE.

FIFTY years of shade and sunshine,
 Fifty years of toil and care,
Fifty years of faithful penance,
 Fifty years of constant prayer!

Solace of the sick and suff'ring,
 Little orphans' loving stay,—
See, in high and holy duties,
 How this brave life passed away.

Crown him (her) with a wreath of roses,
 Blown in purest fields above ;
Ev'ry seed its root reposes
 In some deed of pious love.

While the older friends are praying,
　　Little children shout for glee;
E'en the very saints in heaven
　　Share our Golden Jubilee!

Oh! thou good and faithful servant!
　　May it be thy lot, one day,
In the hour of solemn Judgment,
　　Thus to hear our dear Lord say:

"Come, thou blessed of My Father!
　　Come, my love, and dwell with Me;
Now, at last, we'll keep together
　　Heaven's endless Jubilee!"

Other Tiny Rhymes

FOR

Tiny Readers.

———◆———

I.

With the Babies.

————

Lullaby.

Sleep—sleep—sleep.
　The moon shines brightly,
The yellow stars begin to peep
　The early dew falls lightly;
The lazy, crazy croon
Of crickets 'neath the moon
Is mixing with the tree-frogs' drowsy, tender tune—
　Hush, baby, hush.

Rest—rest—rest.
　　Little sister's dreaming,
Cuddled in her snowy nest,
　　Flaxen hair loose streaming;
Moonlight on the floor
Is tracing o'er and o'er
The vine-leaves, the vine-leaves that tremble 'round
　　the door—
　　　　　　Hush, baby, hush.

Sleep—sleep—sleep.
　　The white cat's purring;
The little mice begin to *cheep*,
　　Behind the wainscot stirring;
The pet canary closes
Its diamond eye, and dozes
In its cage of silver filagree among the sleepy
　　roses—
　　　　　　Hush, baby, hush.

Sleep—sleep—sleep.
　　Evening bells are ringing;
Daisies, where the grass is deep,
　　Fast asleep are swinging;
Near the garden-wall
The lilies rise and fall,
And thou art yet awake, my pet, the sweetest
　　flow'r of all !
　　　　　　Sleep, baby, sleep.
　　　　　　　　　　—E. C. D.

NETTY AND THE ROSES.

OUR sweet little Netty,
So plump and so pretty,
Is safe in her cradle,—God bless her !
And while the pet dozes,
Some red and white roses
Have crept up the wall to caress her.

The white rose is saying,
" To-day I went Maying;
They said that my rose-buds were *stunning ;*
But, sure, my sweet Netty,
They're not half as pretty
As your dear little fingers so cunning !"

The red rose creeps under
The red cheeks with wonder,

And whispers, "What beautiful blushes!
　　Such cheeks, and such lips!
　　One might take them for slips
Of roses that grew on my bushes!"

　　But dear little Netty,
　　So plump and so pretty,
Hears nothing.　Her laughing eye closes,
　　And through the dark hours
　　She sleeps 'mid the flowers,
And dreams about red and white roses.

—E. C. D.

PAPA'S PET.

She looks like her mother,
And you are her brother;
There's ne'er such another
In all the world round.

Her smile is the queerest,
Her eyes are the clearest,
Her face is the dearest,
That ever were found.

— Adapted from "Buds and Flowers."

WAIT!

PATIENTLY dear doggy sits,
Waiting for some little bits;
He likes bread and milk as well
As the little Gabriel.

Wait a bit, you doggy dear,
You shall have some, never fear;
Then we will go out and play
In the field of new-mown hay.

HER FIRST CHRISTMAS.

WHEN BABY LOU HAD A CALL FROM HER BABY
UNCLE, WHOSE BIRTHDAY HAPPENED TO BE CHRIST-
MAS DAY.

FROM her little mamma's knee
Toddles lovely Baby Lou,—
With her mamma's fan, you see,
Makes her bow to Uncle True;

While he waves his hat and brush,
Bows until he nearly falls.
"Come," says Uncle, "do not blush:
Let us play at Christmas-calls."

"Ah! I'm 'most too young to play,
Walk or talk" (says Baby Lou),
"Yet my little heart can say,
Merry Christmas, Uncle True!"

"Wait awhile," says Uncle dear,
"Till a few small years go by,—
There will be no baby here,
But a playmate three feet high!"

" Round the Christmas-tree," says Lou,
" *Then* we'll dance and sing for fun;
Happy birthday, Uncle True,
Merry Christmas, both in one!"

—E. C. D.

THE NEW BABY.

Kiss me, baby, baby boy,
Mother's pet and mother's joy;
Tiny hands so fat and round,
Sweetest darling ever found.

Little hair upon his head,
Round blue eyes, and cheeks so red·
Dimple in his little chin,
You can put your finger in.

Little baby, full of mirth,
Little baby, new to earth;
Say, what dreams of angel joy
Have been thine, my baby boy?

———◆———

FIVE LITTLE CHICKENS.

SAID the first little chicken,
    With a queer little squirm,
" Oh, I wish I could find
    A fat little worm!"

Said the next little chicken,
    With an odd little shrug,
" Oh, I wish I could find
    A fat little bug!"

Said the third little chicken,
    With a sharp little squeal,
" Oh, I wish I could find
    Some nice yellow meal!"

Said the fourth little chicken,
　With a small sigh of grief,
" I wish I could find
　A green little leaf!"

Said the fifth little chicken,
　With a faint little moan,
" I wish I could find
　A wee gravel stone!"

" Now, see here," said the mother,
　From the green garden patch,
" If you want any breakfast,
　You must come and scratch!"

—American Kindergarten Magazine.

NOBODY.

"NOBODY b'oke it! It cracked itself,
It was clear 'way up on the toppest shelf.
I—p'rhaps the kitty-cat knows!"
  Says poor little Ned,
  With his ears as red
As the heart of a damask rose.

"*Nobody* lost it! I carefully
Put my cap where it ought to be
(No, 'tisn't ahind the door),
  And it went and hid,—
  Why, of course it did,
For I've hunted an hour or more."

"*Nobody* tore it! You know things will
Tear if you're sitting just stock-stone still!
I was just jumping over the fence—
  There's some spikes on top,
  And you have to drop
Before you can half commence."

Nobody! wicked Sir Nobody!
Playing such tricks on my children three!
If I but set eyes on you,
  You should find what you have lost,
  But that, to my cost,
I never am like to do!
        —ANNA F. BURNHAM, *in "Wide Awake."*

THE PARROT.

PARROT, parrot, you're talking all day,—
You seem to have terribly much to say :
You shriek and scream, and you squall so loud,
You seem so clever and look so proud ;
But tell me, Polly, and tell me true,
Pray, do you ever learn anything new ?

Mistress Polly, not very well pleased,
Cries, " I won't be questioned, and mocked at, and
    teased.
What do I care for your books and reading ?
Give me fresh biscuits and dainty feeding."
                     —Rhyme and Reason.

FRESH FROM THE FAIR.

TOMMY and Mary have been to the fair,
And what do you think they have brought from
    there ?
A doll, and a donkey that wags his head,
And two great cakes of ginger-bread.
                    —Chimes and Rhymes.

COME HERE, LITTLE ROBIN.

COME here, little Robin,
And don't be afraid;

I would not hurt even a feather.
　Come here, little Robin,
　And pick up some bread
To feed you this very cold weather.

　I don't mean to hurt you,
　You poor little thing !
The pussy-cat is not behind me ;
　So hop about pretty,
　And put down your wing,
And pick up the crumbs, and don't mind me.
　　　　　—Children's Book of Poetry.

MAUD AND MAY.

GUARDIAN angels
　watch must keep
Over Maud and May
　asleep.

Maud her doll was
　holding tight
When she bade us all
　" Good-night !"

Little May " God bless
　me !" said,—
Dropped her ball
　upon the bed.

　　Now they both are sweetly sleeping,
　　And the angels watch are keeping.

When I am Big.

"When I am big,"
  Says little Brown-Hair,
"I'll not play with trumpets,
  Stuck up in a chair.

"When I am big,
  Girl's dresses I'll drop ;
I'll wear coat and pants,
  And a high hat, like Pop.

"When I am big,
A big house I'll build;
With toys, cakes, and candies
The rooms shall be filled.

"When I am big,
A big horse I'll buy,
And over the country,
Like blazes, I'll fly!

"For when I am big,
Dear Pussy, you know,
I'll be a great doctor,
With hair white as snow."

FINGER-SONG.

TO BE SUNG ON BABY'S FINGERS.

One shall have an apple;
Two shall have a pear;
Three shall have a little kid, of which he'll take
good care;
Four shall have some candy;
Five shall have a ride;
Six shall have a little sword, all buckled on his side;
Seven shall have a pony;
Eight shall have a sled;
Nine shall have a dreaming-cap, and *Ten* shall go
to bed.

—*Babyland.*

MY GOOD-FOR-NOTHING.

"WHAT are you good for, my brave little man?
Answer the question for me, if you can—
You, with your fingers as white as a nun;
You, with your ringlets as bright as the sun.
All the day long, with your busy contriving,
Into all mischief and fun you are diving;
See if your wise little noddle can tell
What you are good for.   Now, ponder it well.'

Over the carpet the dear little feet
Came with a patter to climb on my seat;
Two merry eyes, full of frolic and glee,
Under their lashes looked up unto me.
Two little hands, pressing soft on my face,
Drew me down close in a loving embrace;
Two rosy lips gave the answer so true,
"Good to love you, Mamma, good to love you."
                              —EMILY H. MILLER.

THE MOUSE.

I'M only a poor little mouse, ma'am!
I live in the wall of your house, ma'am!
With a fragment of cheese, and a very few peas,
I was having a little carouse, ma'am!

No mischief at all I intend, ma'am!
I hope you will act as my friend, ma'am!
If my life you should take, many hearts it would
    break,
And the trouble would be without end, ma'am!

My wife lives there in the crack, ma'am!
She's waiting for me to come back, ma'am!
She hoped I might find a bit of a rind,
For the children their dinner do lack, ma'am!

'Tis hard living there in the wall, ma'am!
For plaster and mortar will pall, ma'am,
On the minds of the young, and when specially hung-
Ry, upon their poor father they'll fall, ma'am!

I never was given to strife, ma'am!
(Don't look at that terrible knife, ma'am!)
The noise overhead that disturbs you in bed,
'Tis the rats, I will venture my life, ma'am!

In your eyes I see mercy, I'm sure, ma'am!
Oh, there's no need to open the door, ma'am!
I'll slip through the crack, and I'll never come back,
Oh, I'll never come back any more, ma'am!

My Possessions.

I am a rich man,
  If there ever was one:
I've a horse and an apple,
  And both are my own.

But some one might wish
  Such fine presents to keep;
So I'll take them to bed,
  To hold fast while asleep.

And when in the morning
I wake up once more,
I've my toy and my apple,—
To me a rich store.

—Rhyme and Reason.

THE SANDMAN.

HE'S coming, little
    Blue-Eyes,
He's coming up the
    stair,
With his funny tas-
    seled night-cap,
And tufts of snowy
    hair.
Drop your little ruf-
    fled dress,—
Are your shoes un-
    tied?
The Sandman! the
    Sandman
Is on the stairs out-
    side!

His bag's behind his shoulder,
　　He holds his stick before—
I hear him, little Blue-Eyes,
　　He's knocking at the door.
Shake the pillows, Nursey!
　　Baby's fixed for bed—
The Sandman! the Sandman
　　Is poking in his head!

See his pretty flowered coat!
　　Watch his soft old feet!
Round the darling's crib he goes,
　　So sleepy and so sweet!
In between the cosy sheets
　　Blue-Eyes loves to creep—
The Sandman, the Sandman
　　Has put her fast asleep!

　　　　　　　　—E. C. D.

———◆———

THE BABY TELLS WHAT BECAME OF THE LITTLE FISHES.

LITTLE fishes in a brook,
Papa caught them with a hook.

Mamma fried them in a pan,
Papa ate them like a man.

CRADLE-SONG.

SLEEP. baby, sleep!
Thy father watches his sheep;
Thy mother is shaking the dreamland tree,
And down comes a little dream on thee.
Sleep, baby, sleep!

Sleep, baby, sleep!
The large stars are the sheep;
The little stars are the lambs, I guess,
And the gentle moon is the shepherdess.
Sleep, baby, sleep!

Sleep, baby, sleep!
Our Saviour loves His sheep;
He is the Lamb of God on high
Who for our sakes came down to die.
Sleep, baby, sleep!

—Child Life.

"YOU DIRTY BOY!"

"RUB-A-DUB-DUB!"
Cries good Cousin Jane;
"Here's Ted in his tub;
We must bathe him again!

"Dear Martha, come quick !
Bring the water along;
'Twill make the boy sick
If the soap is too strong.

"Now, Ted, we'll begin,--
What a fat little roll !
Oh ! I wish his dear skin
Was as white as his soul !"

II

At Play.

Coasting.

Hurry! skurry! down we go,—
Lots of sunshine, lots of snow!
Am I cold? Oh! no, I'm roasting!
One gets *awful* hot a-coasting!

Say, ain't this a jolly sled?
Papa calls it " *Go-ahead !*"
And go ahead it does, you bet,
Like a race-horse in a pet.

There fly Fred, and little Tim,
And Charley—who's afraid of *him?*
See here, fellows, don't be rough ;
There's room for all, and snow enough.

Bless my stars ! if there ain't Fred
Knocking Charley off his sled !
Both the boys have got a fall—
" *Go-ahead* " has beat them all !

WINTER JEWELS.

A MILLION little diamonds
  Twinkled on the trees,
And all the little maidens said,
  " A jewel, if you please !"

But while they held their hands outstretched
  To catch the diamonds gay,
A million little sunbeams came
  And stole them all away.

—Children's Book of Poetry.

HER LADYSHIP.

THOSE rude little boys,
    They do nothing but stare,
As I ride through the snow
    In my pretty sledge-chair.

My muff and my bonnet,
    They eye them all o'er ;
They can never have seen
    Such a lady before !

—Adapted from " Buds and Flowers."

A New Mother Hubbard.

Miss Polly Betsy Patterson,
  In a Mother Hubbard cloak,
And a Mother Hubbard bonnet
  With a most bewitching poke,

One morning met a curly dog,—
  He was of medium size,
His ears were drooped, his tail was limp,
  And the tears stood in his eyes.

Said Polly to the curly dog,
  "Why do you look so sad ?"
"Because," replied he, with a sniff,
  "The times are very bad.

"You see," said he, "the streets are full
  Of little Mother Hubbards,
But though I've wagged my tail 'most off,
  They never speak of cupboards."

Said Polly Betsy, "Come with me;
  'Twould melt a heart of stone !
I'll give you lots of bread and milk,
  And a juicy mutton-bone."

She took him home, and fed him well;
  His tears were turned to laughter;
And now, wherever Polly goes,
  The curly dog trots after.

      —ELEANOR A. HUNTER, _in " St. Nicholas."_

———◆———

THE GINGERBREAD CAT.

MAMIE had a pussy-cat,
  So well-behaved and sweet,
That all the little children cried,
  "It's good enough to eat !"
It never mewed, nor showed a claw;
  Was never cross or surly;
And Mamie loved it from its ears
  Down to its tail so curly.

This little kitty-cat was brown,
  As brown as brown could be;
But though it had two bright black eyes,
  Alas! it could not see.
And though it had four little paws,
  It couldn't even walk;
And though it had two little ears,
  Could not hear Mamie talk.

And so this helpless pussy-cat
  Much needed special care,
And Mamie kept it in her arms,
  And lugged it everywhere;
Until, alas ! at supper-time,
  This kitty-cat so brown,
Into a bowl of bread and milk
  From Mamie's hand fell down.

So Mamma laid it on the shelf:
  " When morning comes," said she,
" I have no doubt your little puss
  All nice and dry will be."
But such a dreadful thing befell
  The kitty-cat that night !
We know, of course, that cats eat mice,
  A rule that's very right;

But, truly, I am grieved to say,
  This time it was the mice
That put an end to poor Miss Puss,
  And ate her in a trice.
And when the morning dawned, alas !
  All that remained of Kitty
Was just one crumb to tell the tale:
  Now, wasn't that a pity ?

                    —MARY D. BRINE.

I LIKE LITTLE PUSSY.

I LIKE little pussy,
   Her coat is so warm;
And if I don't hurt her
   She'll do me no harm.
So I'll not pull her tail,
   Nor drive her away,
But pussy and I
   Very gently will play;
She shall sit by my side,
   And I'll give her some food;
And she'll love me because
   I am gentle and good.

—JANE TAYLOR.

A Penny to Spend.

They gave me a penny
If I wouldn't cry;
We'll spend it together,
You and I.

Here is a little shop,—
  What shall we take?
There is a beautiful
  Frosted cake.

Cookies in plenty,
  All one needs,
Specked in the middle
  With caraway seeds.

How many buns
  Would a penny buy?
We never can tell
  Until we try.

You must be fair,
  You see, and divide:
I like the ones
  With the cream inside.

A whole bag full!
  Well, that will do.
These are for me—
  That one for you.

—Babyland.

A MAY PARTY.

THE sweet birds are singing,
The young lambs are springing,
The bells are all ringing
    A merry chime.

Then let us go Maying,
For all things are playing ;
In-doors there's no staying
In happy spring-time.

—*Schnick Schnack.*

"GRAN'MA AL'AS DOES."

I WANTS to mend my wagon,
And has to have some nails;
Jus' two, free will be plenty,
We're going to haul our rails.
The splendidest cob fences
We're makin' ever was!
I wis' you'd help us find 'em,
Gran'ma al'as does.

My horse's name is Betsey;
  She jumped and broke her head.
I put her in the stable,
  And fed her milk and bread.
The stable's in the parlor;
  We didn't make no muss :
I wis' you'd let it stay there,
  Gran'ma al'as does.

I wants some bread and butter;
  I's hungry, worstest kind;
But Tatie mustn't have none,
  'Cause she wouldn't mind.
Put plenty sugar on it :
  I tell you what I knows—
It's right to put on sugar,
  Gran'ma al'as does.

———◆———

READING THE NEWS.

THIS milk that I've got
  Is so *awfully* hot,
I must wait till it cools.—What a caper !
  With the dish in my lap,
  I'll just push back my cap,
And see what is fresh in the paper.

Old nurse it will vex
When she misses her specks !
I never intended to fret her;
   I thought I'd just try
   If they suited *my* eye,—
But, bless me ! I can't read a letter !

O mercy ! what's that ?
I declare it's the cat !
(The one we call old Tommy Tupper) :
   While I looked for the news
   He has skipp'd o'er my shoes,
And lapp'd up the whole of my supper !

                 —E. C. D.

GOLD AND GREEN.

GOLD AND GREEN.

GOLD and green and blue and white,
　　Daisies, buttercups, and sky,
Grass and clouds and birds unite
In a chorus of delight :
　　For the tender spring is nigh;
　　Soon will winds no longer sigh.

March and April pass away,
　　And the dainty-fingered rain
Plays sweet melodies all day,
Welcoming the lovely May.
　　Soon will chickweed fill the lane,
　　Poppies sprout amid the grain.
　　　　　　　—MAURICE F. EGAN.

———◆———

WORK AND PLAY.

WORK while you work,
　　Play while you play—
That is the way
　　To be cheerful and gay.

All that you do,
  Do with your might;
Things done by halves
  Are never done right.

One thing at a time,
  And that done well,
Is a very good rule,
  As many can tell.

Moments are useless
  When trifled away ;
So work while you work,
  And play while you play.

An Old Rat's Tale.

He was a rat and she was a rat,
  And down in one house they did dwell ;
And both were as black as a witch's cat,
  And they loved each other right well.

He had a tail and she had a tail,
  Both long and curling and fine ;
And each said, " Yours is the finest tail
  In the world, excepting mine."

He smelt the cheese and she smelt the cheese,
  And they both pronounced it good ;
And they both remarked it would greatly add
  To the charms of their daily food.

So he ventured out and she ventured out,
  And I saw them go with pain ;
But what befell them I never can tell,
  For they never came back again.

  —*St. Nicholas.*

GOOSIE IN THE GARDEN.

Goose, gray goose in the garden,
 Why are you here, I pray?
Your right place is the yard in;
 Goose, gray goose, go away!

Goose, gray goose, look behind you:
　　What if the farmer should see ?
The worse for you, should he find you.—
　　Gray goose, don't hiss at me !

Goose, gray goose, silly rover,
　　Here comes Tom with a switch ;
Hasten and get under cover ;
　　Run down,—hide in the ditch !

*　　　　　　　　　　—Rhyme and Reason.*

———◆———

NAUGHTY NAN.

Little Nan Dunshower
Sat on a sunflower,—
Nursey was hunting all over to find her ;
　　"Ha ! ha !" cried Miss Nanny,
　　"I'll frighten old Fanny ;
She'll think I am lost if I stay here behind her !"

So naughty Nan Dunshower
Hid in the sunflower,
And let her old Nursey go homeward without her;
　　But soon there, benighted,
　　She found, all affrighted,
The leaves were beginning to close up about her !

Alas for Nan Dunshower !
Deep in the sunflower
Vanished her ladyship !   Wasn't it shocking ?
In the morning when Fanny
Came hunting Miss Nanny,
All she could find was a slipper and stocking !

CAMPING OUT.

Down in the garden we've made us a tent
To shut out the sunny blue sky ;
With our books and our toys, and our Mamma's
consent,
We're living there, Clara and I.

'Tis under the rosebush, beside the old fence,
There's beautiful moss on the floor ;
The birdies sing sweet round this nicest of tents,
And the daisies grow thick at the door.

A party we've planned for our Dolly to-day,
The cards to her friends have been sent ;
The dear little darling is in *such* a way,—
Come, look at her here in the tent.

Our china is ready ; we've jelly and cake ;
  And Clarrie is making the tea.
I think you might once, just for dear Dolly's sake,
  Eat supper with Clara and me.

—E. C. D.

THE HORSE-SHOE.

"Good Mr. Smith, I've come to you,
Because my horse has lost its shoe."
   "Pray sir, how did he do it?"
"Why, riding through the Park, one day,
He kicked in such a vicious way,
   That then I think he threw it."

" For ever since he's been quite lame,
So broken-spirited and tame,
 He scarce can whisk his tail."
"Well, Master John, I can't refuse—
I'll make your horse some strong new shoes;—·
 First let me drive this nail."
—Chimes and Rhymes.

---◆---

SONG OF THE PEAR-TREE.

OUT in the green, green meadow
 Standeth a fine pear-tree;
The fine pear-tree hath leaves, too.
 Now what in that bed may be?

  A beautiful child,
  Child in the bed,
  Bed from the feather,
  Feather from the bird,
  Bird from the egg,
  Egg in the nest,
  Nest on the twig,
  Twig on the branch,
  Branch on the tree,
  Tree in the ground.

Out in the green, green meadow
　　Standeth a fine pear-tree;
The fine pear-tree hath leaves, too,
　　And on it these things all be.
　　　　　　　　　　—Rhyme and Reason.

A "FORTY-GRAFF!"

TAKE your picture? Guess I *will;*
Dora, Cora, little Phil,
(Try and keep the baby still!)

Hold your heads up good and high,
Don't you move a hand or eye—
(There! that baby's going to cry!)

Don't you laugh. *This* isn't play;
People always stare away
At the *cam—cam—cameray;*

Look as cross as if they'd crack it,
Just like old Aunt Susan Hackett
In the album on the bracket.

Steady—steady! One—two—three,—
Dora, Cora, Phil,—O see!
No one's *forty-graff'd* but me!

—E. C. D

THE HAY-FIELD.

" Now, youngsters, you may run and play,
And pitch about the new-mown hay;
The day is fair, you're ripe for fun,
So to it, children, every one!"

No second bidding is required,
For every heart with joy is fired;
At once the whole troop bound away,
And toss and tumble in the hay.

Now stifled laughs and mirthful cries
From out one biggish heap arise;
And then pops up that madcap May,
Half-smothered, from the new-mown hay.

—Little Lays for Little Folks

THE LITTLE DRILL-MASTER.

I'D like to be a soldier,
  And wear the red and blue;
I s'pose the shots don't hurt as much
  As people say they do.
My soldiers never mind the peas,
  Although they hit so strong,
And when they fall I pick them up,
  And make them march along.
March along, march along,
Little soldiers, good and strong !

  —Adapted from Coates' Children's Book of Poetry.

DOG AND DOVES.

FLORENCE at the window
  Feeds her doves;
Near her stands dog Fido,
  Whom she loves.

Gentle little Florrie,
  Sweet her words !—
" Come and eat your barley,
  Dearest birds !"

Watching the young mistress
  Whom he loves,
Fido barks, " *She's* sweeter
  Than the doves !"

—E. C. D.

TRUTH.

Boy, at all times tell the truth,
Let no lie defile thy mouth ;
If thou'rt wrong, be still the same—
Speak the truth and bear the blame.

Truth is honest, truth is sure,
Truth is strong and must endure ;
Falsehood lasts a single day,
Then it vanishes away.

Boy, at all times tell the truth,
Let no lie defile thy mouth ;
Truth is steadfast, sure, and fast,
Certain to prevail at last.

———◆———

SULKY JENNY.

JENNY, come again and play,
And don't so sulky be ;
I merely took your ball away
And hid it in a tree.

Lily's waiting at the stile,
In her hand a basket ;
Jenny, raise your head and smile,
Won't you, when I ask it ?

That's right,
Come away ;
Sun's bright,
We will play
Merrily, merrily, all the day !

—Buds and Flowers.

THE LOST CHILD.

"I'M losted!   Could you find me, please?"
   Poor little frightened baby!
The wind had tossed her golden fleece,
The stones had scratched her dimpled knees.
I stooped, and lifted her with ease,
   And softly whispered, "Maybe."

"Tell me your name, my little maid,
   I can't find you without it."
"My name is Shiny-eyes," she said.
"Yes, but your last?"   She shook her head:
"Up to my house 'ey never said
   A single fing about it."

"But, dear," I said, "what is your name?"
   "Why, di'n't you hear me told you?
Dust Shiny-eyes."   A bright thought came:
"Yes, when you're good; but when they blame
You, little one—is't just the same
   When Mamma has to scold you?"

"My mamma never scolds," she moans,
   A little blush ensuing,
"'Cept when I've been a-frowing stones,
And then she says" (the culprit owns),
"'Mehitabel Sapphira Jones,
   What *has* you been a-doing?'"
                              —*Wide Awake.*

A VAIN FROG.

I'M sitting here upon the grass,
  A very charming frog ;
The river is my looking-glass,
  My dressing-room's a log.

I wear a fine green satin coat,
  And vest of speckled silk ;
The necktie round my chubby throat
  Is just as white as milk.

My eyes *are* rather wide apart,
  But, then, how bright they glisten !
And when I sing—why, bless your heart !
  The birds all stop to listen !

—E. C. D.

Santa's Comin'!

Santa's comin'! Guess he is!
   Gran'ma, she's a-knittin'
Biggest stockin' ever was,
   Never needs no fittin'.
She p'tends it's gran'pa's sock ;
   Polly says that's *'post'rous !*—
Says it every bit as if
   Gran'pa was a *'noc'ros !*

Guess I know whose sock it is !
   Guess it's mine for Santa ;
Won't it hold lots ? Hope he knows,
   So he'll bring a plenty ;
Hope he'll cram it from the toe
   To the big red toppin'.
Golly ! Gracious ! Just to think
   Sets a boy a-hoppin' !

Santa's comin' ! Guess he is !
   Mamma smiles at sewin' ;
Everybody all the time
   Looks so awful knowin' ;
'Spose they smell the kitchen things,
   Cakes, and pies, and cheeses.
My ! I feel so good I could
   Hurrah myself to pieces !

— Youth's Companion.

III

A͏t W͏o͏r͏k.

A Queer Kind of School.

Two little fellows, so funny and fat,
One has his Polly, the other his Cat.

Two little teachers, each holding a book;
Polly and Pussy must listen and look!

WHICH LOVED BEST?

A LESSON FOR LITTLE GIRLS THAT NEED NOT BE
DESPISED BY THEIR BIG SISTERS.

"I LOVE you, mother," said little John;
　　Then, forgetting his work, his cap went on,
　　And he was off to the garden-swing,
　　And left her wood and water to bring.

"I love you, mother," said rosy Nell—
"I love you better than tongue can tell."
Then she teased and pouted full half the day,
Till her mother rejoiced when she went to play.

"I love you, mother," said little Fan;
"To-day I'll help you all I can;
How glad I am that school doesn't keep!"
So she rocked the babe till it fell asleep.

Then, stepping softly, she fetched the broom,
And swept the floor, and tidied the room;
Busy and happy all day was she,
Helpful and happy as child could be.

"I love you, mother," again they said—
Three little children going to bed.
How do you think that mother guessed
Which of them really loved her best?

WHAT THE CLOCK SAYS.

THE clock's loud tick
Says, "Time flies quick."
"Listen," says the chime;
"Make the most of time.
For remember, young and old,
Minutes are like grains of gold;
Spend them wisely, spend them well,
For their worth can no man tell!"

"HOLI-O-HO!"

THE GOATHERD'S SONG.

HERE I lie on the top of the hill,
Right glad am I that the wind is still.
I've never a stocking, and never a shoe,
But the grass is green, and the sky is blue;
And clear thro' my dear little horn I blow,
          "Holi-o-ho! holi-o-ho!"

There are violets plenty, and daisies sweet,
Down in the grass at my bare, brown feet;
And my goats are close to my side all day—
White, and dapple, and brown, and gray.
They shake their horns, while *my* horn I blow,
          "Holi-o-ho! holi-o-ho!'

Over my head was a rose-red cloud
When the birds went by in a noisy crowd:
One of them dropped a plume where I sat;
I've fastened it here in the band of my hat.
Once it was high, but now it is low,
          "Holi-o-ho! holi-o-ho!"

Listen, my goats,—ah! well, ah! well,—
Did you hear that sound? 'Tis the vesper-bell.
"Praise God!" 'tis saying, "Praise God again!"
Answer with me, my goats, "Amen!"
I see the spire of the church below,
          "Holi-o-ho! holi-o-ho!"

                    —E. C. D

HOLI-O-HO!

THE CHICKENS.

SEE ! the chickens round the gate
For their morning portion wait ;
Fill the basket from the store,
Let us open wide the door ;
Throw out crumbs and scatter seed,
Let the hungry chickens feed. . . .

Now, my little child, attend :
Your Almighty Father, Friend,
Tho' unseen by mortal eye,
Watches o'er you from on high ;
As the hen her chickens leads,
Shelters, cherishes, and feeds,
So by Him your feet are led,
Over you His wings are spread.

D. A. T.

FOR GOOD AND BAD.

HERE's a slate, its frame is wood ;
  Here's a book,—come, read it.
Here's some fruit for children good,
  And birch for those that need it !

A LITTLE BOY'S TROUBLES.

I THOUGHT when I'd learned my letters
   That all of my troubles were done ;
But I find myself much mistaken—
   They only have just begun.
Learning to read was awful,
   But nothing like learning to write;
I'd be sorry to have you tell it,
   But my copybook is a sight !

The ink gets over my fingers,
   The pen cuts all sorts of shines,
And won't do at all as I bid it;
   The letters won't stay on the lines,
But go up and down and all over,
   As though they were dancing a jig;
They are there in all shapes and sizes—
   Medium, little, and big.

The tails of the g's are con*tra*ry,
   The handles get on the wrong side
Of the d's and the k's and the h's,
   Though I've certainly tried and tried
To make them just right : it is dreadful ;
   I really don't know what to do ;
I'm getting almost distracted;
   My teacher says *she* is, too.

There'd be some comfort in learning
  If one could get through ; instead
Of that, there are books awaiting,
  Quite enough to craze my head.
There's the multiplication-table,
  And grammar, and oh ! dear me,
There's no good place for stopping,
  When one has begun, I see.

My teacher says little by little
  To the mountain-tops we climb ;
It isn't all done in a minute,
  But only a step at a time ;
She says that all the scholars,
  All the wise and learned men,
Had each to begin as I do ;
  If that's so, where's my pen ?

—CARLOTTA PERRY.

SPRING SONG.

THE cock is crowing, the stream is flowing,
The small birds twitter, the lake doth glitter,
  The green field sleeps in the sun ;
The oldest and youngest are at work with the
      strongest;
The cattle are grazing, their heads never raising ;
  There are forty feeding like one !

—WILLIAM WORDSWORTH.

POLLY'S CROSS.

WE'RE keeping school beyond the fence,
We hope to learn much faster.
We're Poll, and Moll,
And Bell, and Nell,
And Jocky,—*he's* the master.

I do *my* best, but Bell and Nell
Will fight with me and Molly;
And Jocky, he
Runs up a tree
And shouts, "Now, ain't this jolly!"

THE GARDENER'S GRANDCHILD.

"WHICH is the queen of the roses ?
  Gardener, can you tell ?"
" Oh, the queen of the roses to me, sir,
  Is my own little grandchild, Nell.

"She waters the flowers for me, sir,
  She carries them out to sell :
Not one is as bright to me, sir,
  As my own little grandchild, Nell.

—From Children's Book of Poetry.

GET UP!

'Tis five o'clock!
Just hear the cock,
How very loud he crows!
Fie, baby Ned,
Don't lie abed,
And take another doze!

'Tis five o'clock!
And this old sock
Is surely out of place;
For sister Jule
Is on the stool
A-sponging off her face.

'Tis five o'clock!
There's Nursey's knock!
Throw pussy-cat a kiss;
Come, baby Ned,
Jump out of bed,
Or breakfast you will miss!

GET UP!

A DOLL IN DISGRACE.

I SIT on my stool
In the midst of my school;
I'm teaching my Pussy to spell.
And when I say " Now! "
She answers " Meow! "
You'd wonder she does it so well.

My Dolly was dumb
When I told her to come,
So I spanked her and put her away;
I have cakes here for Puss,
But Doll made such a fuss
She shan't have a cream-puff to-day.

In the Corn-field.

We've ploughed our land, and with even hand
  The seed o'er the field we've strown;
But sunshine and rain to ripen the grain
  Can be given by God alone.

The seed that springs, and the bird that sings,
  And the shining summer sun ;
The tiny bee and the mighty sea—
  God made them every one.

Then thankful we'll be, for shall not He
  Who gives to each bird a nest,
To each bee a flower for its little hour,
  Give His children food and rest ?

—Children's Book of Poetry.

LEARN YOUR LESSON.

You'll not learn your lesson by crying, my man;
You'll never come at it by crying, my man;
    Not a word can you spy
    For the tear in your eye;
Then set your heart to it, for surely you can.

If you like your lesson, it's sure to like you ;
The words then so quickly would jump into view ·
    Each one to its place
    All the others would chase,
'Till the laddie would wonder how clever he grew.
                —ALEXANDER SMART.

TINY TENDER-HEART.

WITH her yellow garden-hat,
    And her violet gown,
Little Tiny Tender-heart
    Tripped along to town.

In her glove a bright new coin
    Nestled safe and handy—
She was tripping to the store
    For some cakes and candy.

On the road a woman sat,
    By her side a crutch,—
Old and poor !—the silver coin
    Burned in Tiny's clutch !

Just a moment, full of thought,
    Did the maiden stand,
Then she came and dropped her coin
    In the beggar's hand !

Little Tiny Tender-heart
  Shook her curls so brown,
In her pretty garden-hat,
  Tripped *away* from town.

Though of sweetmeats she had none
  On that blessèd day,—
Thinking where her coin had gone,
  She was bright and gay.

All the candy in the shop,
  All the sweetest cake,
Were not sweeter than her deed
  Done for God's dear sake !

—E. C. D.

———◆———

THE BIRDS.

Who taught you to sing,
  My sweet, pretty birds?
Who tuned your beautiful throats?
  You make all the woods
    And the valleys to ring,
  You bring the first news
    Of the earliest spring,
With your loud and silvery notes.

"It was God," said a lark,
  As he rose from the earth :
"*He* gives us the good we enjoy ;
  He painted our wings,
    He gave us our voice,
    He finds us our food,
    He bids us rejoice ;—
Good-morning, my beautiful boy !"
                    —Mrs. Sigourney.

GLAD TO GET OFF.

I NEVER saw such letters,
   They put me in a rage !—
I'd rather catch a dozen mice
   Than read another page.

I wish I had a sup of cream,
   Or just a bite of cheese.
There goes a mouse behind that screen !—
   Excuse me, if ou please.

ROSES RED AND LILIES WHITE.

ROSES red and lilies fair,
  Daisies in a row,
Woodbine sweet and pansies rare,
  In my garden grow.

Little blue forget-me-not,
  With its yellow eye,
Always smiles and gives a nod
  As I pass it by.

Violets play at hide-and-seek,
  But I find them out ;
Underneath their leaves they keep,
  And watch what I'm about.

Ah! 'tis very nice to work
  With dear little Joe,—
Such a lot of pretty flow'rs
  In my garden grow!
                    —*Altered from "Schnick-Schnack."*

TWO AND ONE.

Two ears and only *one mouth* have you ;
  The reason, I think, is clear :
It teaches, my child, that it will not do
  To *talk* about all you *hear*.

Two eyes and only *one mouth* have you ;
  The reason of this must be :
That you should learn that it will not do
  To *talk* about all you *see*.

Two hands and only *one mouth* have you,
  And it is worth while repeating :
The *two* are for work you will have to do—
  The *one* is enough for eating.
                    —*Children's Book of Poetry.*

IV.

AT PRAYER.

A Little Boy's Morning Hymn.

Little Jesus, Babe Divine,
Take my heart and make it Thine.

Fill it full of love for Thee,
Do not let me naughty be.

And since Thou wert once a child,
Make me now both pure and mild.

—E. C. D.

The Guardian Angel.

Dear Angel ! ever at my side,
  How loving must thou be,
To leave thy home in heaven to guard
  A little child like me.

I cannot feel thee touch my hand
  With pressure light and mild,
To check me, as my mother does,
  When I'm a naughty child.

But I have felt thee in my thoughts,
  Fighting with sin for me ;
And when my heart loves God, I know
  The sweetness is from thee.

Yes ! when I pray, thou prayest too—
  Thy prayer is all for me ;
But when I sleep, thou sleepest not,
  But watchest patiently.

Then love me, love me, Angel dear,
   And I will love thee more ;
And help me when my soul is cast
   Upon the eternal shore.

               —Fr. Faber.

HOLY COMMUNION.

CAN it be that my God
  Comes down from heaven?
Makes my heart His abode
  To me is given?
Yes, yes, within my breast
Soon shall my Jesus rest;
Soon shall He be my guest,
  Nor thence be driven.

Then, O my Jesus, come,
  Come to this dwelling;
Make my poor heart Thy home,
  Make Thine each feeling.
Still, still, my blessed God!
Feed me with this sweet food;
Still with Thy sacred Blood
  All my wounds healing.

———◆———

GRACE BEFORE MEALS.

DINNER'S on the table,
  Children take their place;
Each one who is able
  Listens to the grace.

Even little baby
Folds her tiny hands ;
See, she listens,—maybe
She, too, understands.

THE GRACE.

" Lord, that givest all things good,
To whom the ravens look for food,
Deign to look on us from heaven,
And bless the food that Thou hast given."

—Rhyme and Reason.

A Little Girl's Hymn to the Blessed Virgin.

Sweet Virgin Mary !
Oh ! watch over me ;
Guide my bark safely
Through Life's troubled sea.

And when in sorrow,
List to my prayer ;
Cherish me, love me,
With motherly care.

And should I wander
　From truth and from right,
Lead me, O Mary !
　Through Sin's gloomy night.

Teach me to love Him
　Who died for mankind ;
Teach me to banish
　Self-love from my mind.

Be with me, Mother,
　At the hour of death,—
" Jesus and Mary !"
　Shall be my last breath !

　　　—*Composed by E. C. D. at the age of nine years.*

THE GUARDIAN ANGEL TO THE LITTLE GIRLS.

WHAT should a little girl be, friends?
What should a little girl be?
   An innocent child,
   With a heart undefiled,
And a conscience unspotted and free.

Not a mere puppet for show, friends,
Not a mere puppet for show ;
  With manners as old,
  And spirit as cold
As a woman of forty or so.

Not a wild, boisterous girl, friends,—
A thoughtless and boisterous girl,
  With a rude, bold tread,
  And an empty head,
And a lip which does nothing but curl.

But pure should a little girl be, friends,
A violet shrinking from sight ;
  Like Mary, the meek,
  With a blush on her cheek.
And the robe of her soul ever white.

And through the dark winter of life, friends,
The gloomy and dangerous way,
  The freshness of spring
  Around her will cling,
Till the gold of her tresses turns gray.

And then, as a favorite child, friends
(All failures and frailties forgiven),
  She will fly, without dread,
  To that God who hath said :
"Of *such* is the Kingdom of Heaven !"

                —E. C. D.

A Child's Evening Prayer.

Ere on my bed my limbs I lay,
God grant me grace my prayers to say.
O God, preserve my mother dear
In strength and health for many a year ;
And oh ! preserve my father too,
And may I pay him reverence due ;
And may I my best thoughts employ
To be my parents' hope and joy.

And oh ! preserve my brothers both
From evil doings and from sloth ;
And may we always love each other,
Our friends, our father, and our mother.
And still, O Lord, to me impart
An innocent and grateful heart,
That, after my last sleep, I may
Awake to Thy eternal day !

Amen.

(Composed by the poet Coleridge for his little daughter)
—From Coates' Children's Book of Poetry.

MORNING HYMN FOR A LITTLE GIRL.

LOVING Mother, look, I pray,
On thy little girl to-day.
Undefiled and meek, like thee,
She would ever, ever be.
Sweet and gentle, pure and mild,
Ever like thy Holy Child.